The Adventures of "BOCHO"

By John & Sally Jenkins

AuthorHouse™
1663 Liberty Drive
Bloomington, IN 47403
www.authorhouse.com
Phone: 1 (800) 839-8640

Published by AuthorHouse 11/27/2017

ISBN: 978-1-5462-1905-7 (sc)
ISBN: 978-1-5462-1906-4 (e)

Print information available on the last page.

authorHOUSE®

BOCHO : I want to tell you a little story about my life. My name is Bocho. I am a puppy. I won't start my story with, "Once upon a time", because this story that I am going to tell you is basically a true story.

Being Born: *It's hot and dark in here. What do I keep bumping into. It is surely crowded and getting more crowded every day. I wonder what is happening. Everything is kind of shaking, and I'm afraid. There is an opening up ahead. It seems too small for me to slide through, but I think that is what is going to happen. Wow, I got through but hit the floor pretty hard. Here comes another puppy, and another, and another, and another. Let me count. I have two sisters and four brothers, plus me. That makes seven of us in all.*

I can hardly see. It is so hard to get my eyes open, but boy is it bright out here. I like it, but I'm getting hungry. I think that I am supposed to eat from momma's spigots. There are enough spigots so all of us can eat at the same time. Boy the milk in momma's spigots tastes really good. The milk filled my tummy and makes me so sleepy. ZZZZZZ.

Finding Homes: *It is fun to play with my brothers and sisters. We run and play all day long and have so much fun. Something in my belly hurts. Our friend puts us in a basket and takes us out into the city. People come by and are taking my brothers and sisters to their homes. Oh, here comes a beautiful girl looking for one of us for her home. Boy is she pretty. I hope she picks me.*

She chose me and took me with her. I don't feel very good though, my tummy really hurts. The beautiful lady wants to play, but I don't want to do anything but sleep. I don't feel very good. She says I must be sick and she took me to the doctor. He said I was really sick, and gave me some medicine. He said I needed to stay with him overnight, so he could watch me and maybe give me more medicine. I have begun to feel some better but still have to stay another day. By the end of the second day, the beautiful lady came and took me home with her. I heard the doctor say that I wouldn't have made it if she hadn't brought me in. I feel all better now, and I'm so happy.

New Momma: She is nice, and we play and play. She took me with her when she went to get me a beautiful red collar and leash. I heard her friends calling her Jamie. That must be her name. We played and played and played, and I really had a good time with her. I am so happy that she decided to become my new momma.

We go for walks every day which gives me a chance to tinkle. I love going for walks and I love to tinkle. We get to meet other people and sometimes we get to meet other dogs which is what I really like. A puppy greets another dog by growling and barking a little and later we like to sniff each other. Another thing that I really like to do is smell and sniff hydrants, trees, bushes, and walls. The fun is to see if any other dog has tinkled on them before I got there.

I Go To Work:
Jamie takes me to work with her. She just puts me in her purse and away we go. She lets me out occasionally to walk around and I usually tinkle on the floor a time or two. Jamie quickly wipes it up before anyone else sees it. I still sleep a lot as I am just a puppy. I just crawl into her purse to sleep. I am still very small, but very noisy in a ruff-ruff sort of way.

I really like the people in the place where Jamie lives. They make over me and always want to pat me and stuff, and I want as much of that as I can get. Jamie just leaves me with them when she has to go where I cannot go. Everyone seems to love having me around, because I am so cute, at least that is what they keep saying about me.

Going Home: *I have had a really good time in Bolivia, South America. I am a puppy and everyone loves a puppy. Soon, Jamie began to talk about going home because her job in Bolivia was finished. I don't know what it means to go home, but Jamie seems to be excited about it. Jamie has become very busy preparing for our trip. Her friends kept having parties for her saying good-bye and hugging and crying. I don't understand why everyone is crying so much.*

Puppy School: *One thing that I will always remember about Bolivia is the time I spent at the "make believe" Puppy School. One of the memorable things that I remember is that it was all in Spanish. They told us to constantly wag our tails because that always helps to make friends. We didn't learn much about begging, because we will learn more about that in the advanced classes.*

Tall: *Everyone is so tall. It's hard for me to see clear up to momma's face, but momma sits on the floor to play with me. It scares me to play when there are a lot of people around. I am afraid that someone won't see me and will accidentally step on me. I bark and growl a lot to let people know that I am down here.*

Plane: Jamie got ready to make the trip home. She took one bag for her things plus one small box for me. My box had holes in it so I could breathe.

I gladly jumped in the box for our trip. Momma carried me a long way toward this great big blue and white thing. I found out that it was called an airplane. She had to do a lot of things before we could get on the plane. Many people got on the plane before us, but finally we got to get on. Momma found a place to sit down, and she put me in my box under her seat.

I thought this was going to be fun, but momma kept rubbing some stuff on my nose and every time she did, "boom"I went to sleep. All of a sudden, I was awakened by the huge roar of the plane. The plane started to move and the roar got even louder. We started moving real fast and the plane left the ground and began to fly up into the beautiful blue sky. I started to cry softly and guess what, momma put some more stuff on my nose and "boom," ZZZZZZZZZZ.

Every time I began to wake up, "boom" she put that stuff on my nose again. After what seemed to be a long time, the plane landed. There were many, many people checking everything. They didn't check me, however. We walked a long way before we got away from the plane.Jamie let me run and play in the airport. Soon, however, we had to get back on another plane. Guess what, no sooner than I got in my box, "boom" Jamie put that stuff on my nose again, ZZZZZZZZ.

Ohio: Soon, the plane landed and again, it took forever to get away from the airport. Jamie carried me. We got to meet Jamie's mom and dad. I thought Jamie was tall but when I met her dad, I couldn't even begin to see his head. Her mom was beautiful just like Jamie.

We went to their home. They have a concrete pond which they call a swimming pool. It was summertime and everyone wanted to go swimming but me.

Every once in a while, however, someone would throw me into the water. YUCK!!! I don't like to swim. They had a funny thing in their doors. They had doggy doors in both doors to the outside which means I could go inside or outside by myself whenever I wanted. Wow what a nice place. There was a huge fenced in yard where I could run and play and be safe.

Philadelphia: After about a week, Jamie took me to her home, in Philadelphia. She had a nice apartment. Jamie had to go to work every day, and boy did I miss her, but when she came home, we always went for a long walk. I really enjoyed those walks.

We traveled down a nice street and on to a nice park. The park had lots of grass, people, benches, and other dogs. What a blast! How could I ask for anything any better than that?

Jamie had lots of friends, and I was so happy to see them come to visit. Once Jamie had a friend come to live with her for a while. She was mean to me from the start. I fixed her though. I tinkled on her blanket as often as I could. Jamie scolded me, but I think she was happy that I had tinkled on her friends blanket, because Jamie was finally ready for her to leave, too.

Ecuador:
Later, Jamie's work was transferred from Philadelphia to Ecuador, South America. She was offered a great opportunity, so we began to prepare to go. She purchased a larger box than the one we used to come to America, because I was getting bigger. When checking about tickets, Jamie found out that I could not go with her. This time, I would be required to travel in the belly of the plane in the baggage area. The only problem with that was the temperature in the belly of the plane would be about 20*, and that is just too cold for me to survive. Jamie had a decision to make, but all she could do was cry. She regretfully decided to leave me with grand-ma and grand-pa, back in Ohio.

Jamie didn't have time to take me to grand-ma and grand-pa's so she sent me on a bus all by myself. I was so afraid. I missed Jamie and I didn't know where I was going. I cried and cried until I finally went to sleep. We traveled for a long time. Finally, we stopped, and they put my cage on a table. I didn't have to stay there long because grand-ma and grand-pa came to get me. Jamie had put my leash in the cage. Grand-ma put the leash on me and took me for a walk. Oh! Wow! I got to tinkle in a new place. I was so excited. After my walk, we got into their car to go to their house. I remembered the doggy doors and went out in the back yard. I didn't know it, but I was home.

Bi-lingual:
When everyone, relatives and friends came to visit us, they were amazed that the only language I understood was Spanish. When kids came to visit, they loved to say Spanish words to me, so I would do their commands. They were always happy to show others how I understood Spanish. I quickly learned

the English commands too, so I became bi-lingual. Wow, I guess I'm pretty special!!! I can understand Spanish and English.

They Treat Me Nice: *I always try to be nice and obey grand-ma and grand-pa. They always treat me good, too. They let me sleep with them. I spent a lot of time on grand-pa's lap watching TV. They always had food and fresh water available for me. They often had folks over for me to visit with. I am happy living here.*

Fishing: *One day when I went with grand-ma and grand-pa fishing, I played and had a great time sniffing everything, until a great big ugly dog came by and scared me a bunch. I immediately jumped on grand-pa's lap and of course he protected me until the big dog left. I was really afraid.*

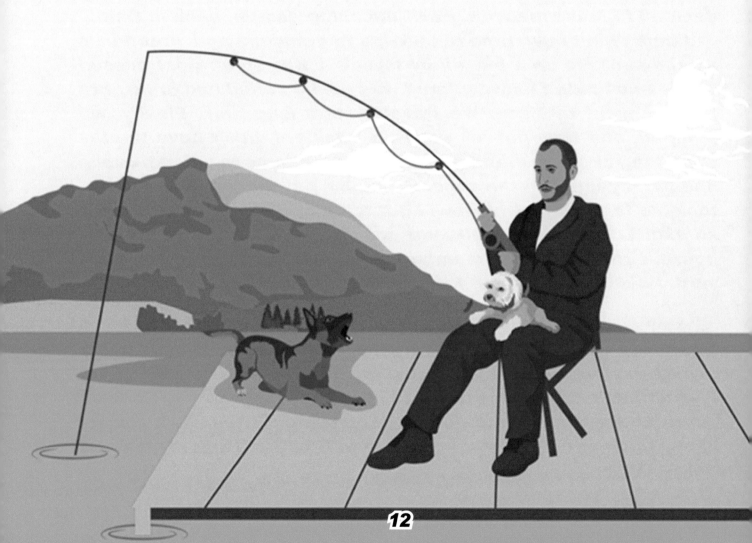

Poison: One day I was going through the garage. I saw and smelled something real good and sweet. I went over to the cabinet to find that blue pills had fallen on the floor. I quickly ate some of them and they tasted real good, so I ate some more. My tummy started to hurt really badly though. I began to froth at the mouth. Grand-pa found me and looked around to see what I had gotten into. He saw the rat poison on the floor and knew I had eaten some of it.

Grand-pa asked grand-ma to call our veterinarian to find out what to do while he held me. The vet told her to pour pure hydrogen peroxide down my throat to make me vomit. Grand-pa grabbed me and grand-ma held my head while they poured the peroxide down my throat. Grand-ma and grand-pa just cried and cried. It was awful for all of us, but I began to vomit everything out of my stomach. Oh, I didn't feel very good. I must have vomited all the poison out of my stomach since I didn't die, but boy did I feel terrible. It wasn't long though until I began to feel real good again and was back to my old self.

Grooming:

They have always kept me groomed. My hair is thick, white, and curly and would get pretty long and turn light brown if I didn't get a haircut. The first time I was trimmed, the trimmer didn't know how to trim a dog like me. She basically shaved me bald. I was so embarrassed, I didn't want anybody to see me, and I tried to hide. It took three months, however, for my hair to grow back out. Grand-ma really checked out every possible groomer until she finally found Mary Beth. She did an excellent job, and I looked great. She put a very fragrant talcum powder on me. I smelled really goooooood. She tied a pretty scarf around my neck which I absolutely loved. I went to her every time I needed a trim and wash for years, and she always did a nice job. I always felt so good about myself.

Once when I went for a trim, Mary Beth was real busy, and she had a very young assistant trim me. It was terrible. She cut my tear ducts in my eyes. which made my eyes weep 24/7, and still leaves dark wet marks under my eyes. Grand-pa made sure that the only person allowed to give me a trim, after that was Mary Beth.

Although, I love to be trimmed up nicely, the process of getting trimmed is a little tough. First I have to be bathed. YUCK!!! I hate the water. I have to have my whole body under water except for my head to kill any fleas that I may have. Then she washes me. Rub a dub-dub with special soap that really gets me clean. I feel so much better since I don't smell so bad anymore. Then she takes me out of the water, and I about freeze until she gets me under the hair dryer. Now I am getting nice and warm, and it is time to be trimmed. The hum of the razor and the hair falling off of me is such a good feeling. There is hair everywhere. Mary Beth cleans it up before finishing me. Snip, snip, snip as the scissors begin to finish the job. I get so excited knowing how good I am going to look. Soon it will be time for grand-ma and grand-pa to come and pick me up. They get so excited. They just go on and on about how good I look and smell, and It makes me feel goooood too.

Car Ride: *Another real treat for me was to get to go in the car, no matter where we were going. We eat out a lot and every time we do, they get me a treat. Usually a cheeseburger for me minus the onions, and pickle of course. We have ice cream too, and often we would go to the park for a picnic. The park is beautiful and has many places for me to enjoy. I enjoy sniffing and the park is just full of different kinds of stuff to sniff. One time, we traveled 200 miles to visit grand-pa's sister. She was nice and had a huge back yard that was fenced in and had many, many posts holding up the wire fencing. I decided that I would not be a happy camper until I had tinkled on each one. Boy was that fun.*

Thor: My life was perfect until "Thor" happened. Grand-ma and grand-pa's son, Scott brought a dog by, that his family couldn't handle any more. I don't know why grand-ma and grand-pa were asked to keep him, but here he came. Thor was huge and a real bully. His breed was a boxer. He would just shove me around for the fun of it. I always wanted to go hide. Grand-pa and grand-ma wouldn't let Thor hurt me when they saw him do things, but they weren't always around. It was fun for me to play outside with him though, because I was so much faster and quicker than he was. I ran circles around him. I could run and hide. Inside, I didn't have many places to hide, and I couldn't get away so easily. I would put up with his foolishness until I just couldn't stand it anymore. Then, I would climb on Thor's back, bite his ears, bark and growl at him. That always slowed him down for a while. One day Thor got very sick though and died. I didn't like Thor, because he was so mean, but I didn't want anything to happen to him. I sure didn't want him to die. I was real sad for days. Even though he was big and rough, we were still friends, and I miss him.

Teddy: *I do have another real good friend. His name is Teddy. He is a little black poodle. He is actually my cousin. He's a country dog but real nice. It's fun to go to his house as he gets to run wild all over the neighborhood. We go play across the road until grand-pa realizes where I have gone. Boy does grand-pa get mad with me, because he's afraid for me to cross a busy road. He makes me stay in the car for the rest of our visit. When we get to play inside though, we really have a great time. We play tag and rip and race all over his huge house. They have three levels, and we race through all of them. What fun we have playing tag. We play for hours and hours. Teddy is so much fun!*

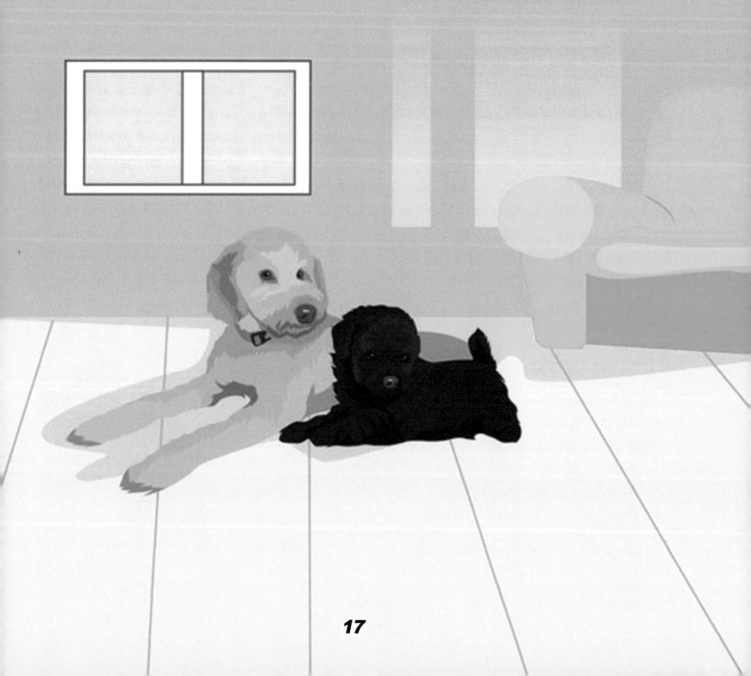

17

Age: I am now 12 years old in human years, which is 84 years old in doggie years. I get around pretty well. I can still jump on the bed carrying my stuffed doggie. I insist that grand-ma take me outside through the office door some times. I can still jump into the car without help. I love to run and play in the back yard. I really love to chase the bunnies and moles. I catch one now and then and play with it for quite a while. I hold it in my mouth and let it loose long enough to play with it. Eventually, it dies from being in my mouth. I really do not mean to hurt it. I just want to play with it. Many times, I will bring them indoors and play with them in the house on the carpet until grand-ma or grand-pa discover them and then, they pick them up and throw them out in the front yard where I cannot go.

Little Beggar: I really enjoyed "make believe" puppy school which didn't last long. Puppy school taught me to get things that I wanted when grand-ma and grand-pa really didn't want me to have them. One of the most important things that is learned in puppy school is how to beg. Thor was the best beggar that I have ever seen. When begging one needs to stare at the adults for many, many minutes. Seldom can they resist if the begging goes on for a long time. I like to stare at grand-ma so she will go outside with me. If I stare and beg long enough, she always comes to the door and goes out with me. I love to be outside when someone is with me. Part of my best begging I learned from Thor.

Key Words: Some of the key words that I recognize are: going, go, someone is coming, who is that, we'll be back soon, sit, Bocho, in a minute, come on, that's all, shake and etc. It's fun to understand all these words.

Hero: *Once when grand-ma went out with me, we went out to the gazebo as she always worked with the pool pump, but this time she slipped and fell and hit her head on the pump. She didn't get up, so I went to her and licked and kissed her head. She still didn't move at all. I was afraid, because she never did that before. I stayed with her until I really became afraid for her. I went in to tell grand-pa. I went in and barked, and just fussed and fussed and finally got grand-pa to realize that something was wrong. He followed me outside and saw grand-ma. He as quickly as he could went over to her and immediately called 911 for help.*

Pretty soon, a noisy truck arrived. They put grand-ma on a stretcher and took her in the truck. Grand-pa jumped into the truck too, and off they went to the hospital. Grand-ma stayed at the hospital for two days. Finally she came home and looked pretty good except for the scratch on her head. She is all better now. They tell me that I am a HERO. I am not a HERO. I would have done anything to help grand-ma.

I Don't Mind As Well: *As I get older, I do not listen as well. I come when grand-pa calls, but in my own good time. Sometimes I sneak out and run across the busy, busy highway. I know it's wrong, but I cannot seem to stop myself. I do more things where I might get hurt.*

Love: *My life with grand-ma and grand-pa is wonderful. They have never ever hit me or hurt me. They constantly try to help me to enjoy my life with them. They take me out for a ride nearly every day. They almost always get me some kind of treat while we are out. They always have me groomed and love me so much. They have made me feel like family all my life. I am so lucky to have them as my family. I love you grand-ma and grand-pa. You guys are the best. You have made my life complete, and I thank you.*

Finis

19

About the Authors: The authors of the book "Bocho" have roots in Appalachia. They have an honor system built into them from their heritage. They believe in the institution of marriage, and they have been married to each other for fifty- seven years. They are ingrained with the importance of manners, respect, common sense, patience, integrity, morals, character, trust, and love. Their thinking is based on their values, in order of importance: GOD, Family, and Country.

GOD: The authors have an overwhelming belief in the hereafter and that GOD is in control!!!

Family: We believe that much of the strength of our nation is based on the cohesiveness of our families. Each member of the family should be completely loyal to each other, to their faith, and to their country. We will always stand for our national anthem and our flag, and wonder about those who do not.

Country: We live in the greatest country in the world. GOD has blessed us with much. It is important for us to use these gifts wisely: Faith, Power, & Environment. We have strong beliefs in our symbols like the flag, national anthem, armed forces, and veterans. Our HERO'S are our veterans and our present uniformed military people.

The book "Bocho" is written about a little fellow that has been a real friend and family member of ours. He has always been a perfect gentleman to our family and friends. This book is written to emphasize our devoted love for this little guy and to highlight the love that your pet may have had or is to you.

Printed in the United States
By Bookmasters